Published by Creative Education, Inc.
123 S. Broad Street, Mankato, Minnesota 56001

Designed by Rita Marshall
Cover Illustration by Etienne Delessert

Library of Congress Cataloging-in-Publication Data

Maupassant, Guy de, 1850–1893.
  [Ficelle. English]
  The string/by Guy de Maupassant.
  p.  cm.
  Translation of: La ficelle.
  Summary: A simple peasant has his life destroyed by the lie of an
enemy who accuses him of a theft.
  ISBN 0-88682-297-1
  [1. Honesty—Fiction.  I. Title.
PZ7.M44515St  1989
[Fic]—dc20                                    89-37306
                                                 CIP
                                                 AC

# THE
# STRING

GUY DE
MAUPASSANT

CREATIVE EDUCATION INC.

ALONG ALL THE ROADS AROUND

GODERVILLE THE PEASANTS AND THEIR

*wives were coming toward the little town, for it*

*was market-day. The men walked with slow*

*steps, their whole bodies bent forward at each*

*movement of their long twisted legs, deformed*

*by their hard work, by the weight on the plough*

which, at the same time, raises the left shoulder

and distorts the figure, by the reaping of the

wheat which forces the knees apart to get a firm

stand, by all the slow and painful labors of the

country. Their blouses, blue, starched, shining as

if varnished, ornamented with a little design in

white at the neck and wrists, puffed about their

bony bodies, seemed like balloons ready to carry

*them off. From each of them a head, two arms,*

*and two feet protruded.*

Some led a cow or a calf at the end of a rope, and their wives, walking behind the animal, whipped its haunches with a leafy branch to hasten its progress. They carried on their arms large wicker-baskets, out of which a chicken here, a duck there, thrust out its head. And they walked with a quicker, livelier step than their husbands. Their spare, straight figures were wrapped in a scanty little shawl, pinned over their flat bosoms, and their heads were envel-

oped in a piece of white linen tightly pressed on

the hair and surmounted by a cap.

~~~~~~~~~~~~~~~~~~~~ Then a wagon passed, its

nag's jerky trot shaking up and down two men

seated side by side and a woman in the bottom

of the vehicle, the latter holding on to the sides

to lessen the hard jolts.

In the square of Goderville there was a

crowd, a throng of human beings and animals

mixed together. The horns of the cattle, the

rough-napped top-hats of the rich peasants, and

the head-gear of the peasant women rose above

the surface of the crowd. And the clamorous, shrill, screaming voices made a continuous and savage din which sometimes was dominated by the robust lungs of some countryman's laugh, of the long lowing of a cow tied to the wall of a house.

It all smacked of the stable, the dairy, and the dung-heap, of hay and sweat, giving forth that sharp, unpleasant odor, human and animal, peculiar to the people of the fields.

Maître Hauchecorne, of Bréauté, had just arrived at Goderville, and was directing his steps toward the square, when he perceived upon the ground a little piece of string. Maître Hauche-corne, economical like a true Norman, thought that everything useful ought to be picked up, and he stooped painfully, for he suffered from rheumatism. He took the bit of thin cord from the ground and was beginning to roll it carefully when he noticed Maître Malandain, the harness-maker, on the threshold of his door, looking at him. They had once had a quarrel together on the subject of a halter, and they had remained on bad terms, being both good haters. Maître Hauchecorne was seized with a sort of shame to be seen thus by his enemy, picking a bit of string out of the dirt. He concealed his find quickly under his blouse, then in his trousers pocket; then he pretended to be still looking on the ground for something which he did not find, and he went towards the market, his head thrust forward, bent double by his pains.

He was soon lost in the noisy and slowly moving crowd, which was busy with interminable bargainings. The peasants looked at cows, went away, came back, perplexed, always in fear of being cheated, not daring to decide, watching the vendor's eye, ever trying to find the trick in the man and the flaw in the beast.

The women, having placed their great baskets at their feet, had taken out the poultry, which lay upon the ground, tied together by the feet, with terrified eyes and scarlet crests.

They heard offers, stated their prices with a dry air and impassive face, or perhaps, suddenly deciding on some proposed reduction, shouted to the customer who was slowly going away: "All right, Maître Anthime, I'll give it to you for that."

Then little by little the square was deserted, the Angelus rang for noon, and those who lived too far away went to the different inns.

At Jourdain's the great room was full of people eating, as the big yard was full of vehicles of all kinds, carts, gigs, wagons, nondescript carts, yellow with dirt, mended and patched, raising their shafts to the sky like two arms, or perhaps with their shafts on the ground and their backs in the air.

Right against the diners seated at the table, the immense fireplace, filled with bright flames, cast a lively heat on the backs of the row on the right. Three spits were turning on which were chickens, pigeons, and legs of mutton; and an appetizing odor of roast meat and gravy dripping over the nicely browned skin rose from the hearth, lightened hearts and made mouths water.

All the aristocracy of the plough ate there, at Maître Jourdain's, tavern keeper and horse dealer, a clever fellow who had money.

The dishes were passed and emptied, as were the jugs of yellow cider. Every one told his affairs, his purchases, and sales. They discussed the crops. The weather was favorable for the greens but rather damp for the wheat.

Suddenly the drum began to beat in the yard, before the house. Everybody rose, except a few indifferent persons, and ran to the door, or to the windows, their mouths still full, their napkins in their hands.

After the public crier had stopped beating his drum, he called out in a jerky voice, speaking his phrases irregularly:

"It is hereby made known to the inhabitants of Goderville, and in general to all persons present at the market, that there was lost this morning, on the road to Benzeville, between nine and ten o'clock, a black leather pocketbook containing five hundred francs and some business papers. The finder is requested to return same to the Mayor's office or to Maître Fortuné Houlbrèque of Manneville. There will be twenty francs reward."

Then the man went away. The heavy roll of the drum and the crier's voice were again heard at a distance.

Then they began to talk of this event discussing the chances that Maître Houlbrèque had of finding or not finding his pocket-book.

And the meal concluded. They were finishing their coffee when the chief of the gendarmes appeared upon the threshold.

He inquired:

"Is Maître Hauchecorne, of Bréauté, here?"

Maître Hauchecorne, seated at the other end of the table, replied:

"Here I am."

And the officer resumed:

"Maître Hauchecorne, will you have the goodness to accompany me to the Mayor's office? The Mayor would like to talk to you."

The peasant, surprised and disturbed, swallowed at a draught his tiny glass of brandy, rose, even more bent than in the morning, for the first steps after each rest were specially difficult, and set out, repeating: "Here I am, here I am."

The Mayor was awaiting him, seated in an armchair. He was the local lawyer, a stout, serious man, fond of pompous phrases.

"Maître Hauchecorne," said he, "you were seen this morning picking up, on the road to Benzeville, the pocket-book lost by Maître Houlbrèque, of Manneville."

The countryman looked at the Mayor in astonishment, already terrified by this suspicion resting on him without his knowing why.

"Me? Me? I picked up the pocket-book?"

"Yes, you, yourself."

"On my word of honor, I never heard of it."

"But you were seen."

"I was seen, me? Who says he saw me?"

"Monsieur Malandain, the harness-maker."

The old man remembered, understood, and flushed with anger.

"Ah, he saw me, the clodhopper, he saw me pick up this string, here, Mayor." And rummaging in his pocket he drew out the little piece of string.

"You will not make me believe, Maître Hauchecorne, that Monsieur Malandain, who is a man we can believe, mistook this cord for a pocket-book."

The peasant, furious, lifted his hand, spat at one side to attest his honor, repeating:

"It is nevertheless God's own truth, the sacred truth. I repeat it on my soul and my salvation."

The Mayor resumed:

"After picking up the object, you stood like a stilt, looking a long while in the mud to see if any piece of money had fallen out."

The old fellow choked with indignation and fear.

"How anyone can tell—how anyone can tell

—such lies to take away an honest man's repu-
tation! How can anyone——"

There was no use in his protesting, nobody
believed him. He was confronted with Monsieur Malandain, who repeated and maintained
his affirmation. They abused each other for an
hour. At his own request, Maître Hauchecorne
was searched. Nothing was found on him.

Finally the Mayor, very much perplexed, dis-
charged him with the warning that he would
consult the Public Prosecutor and ask for fur-
ther orders.

The news had spread. As he left the Mayor's office, the old man was surrounded and questioned with a serious or bantering curiosity, in which there was no indignation. He began to tell the story of the string. No one believed him. They laughed at him.

He went along, stopping his friends, beginning endlessly his statement and his protestations, showing his pockets turned inside out, to prove that he had nothing.

They said:

"Ah, you old devil!"

And he grew angry, becoming exasperated, hot, and distressed at not being believed, not knowing what to do and always repeating himself.

Night came. He had to leave. He started on his way with three neighbors to whom he pointed out the place where he had picked up the bit of string; and all along the road he spoke of his adventure.

In the evening he took a turn in the village of Bréauté, in order to tell it to everybody. He only met with incredulity.

It made him ill all night.

The next day about one o'clock in the after-
noon, Marius Paumelle, a hired man in the
employ of Maître Breton, husbandman at
Ymauville, returned the pocket-book and its
contents to Maître Houlbrèque of Manneville.

This man claimed to have found the object in
the road; but not knowing how to read, he had
carried it to the house and given it to his em-
ployer.

The news spread through the neighborhood.
Maître Hauchecorne was informed of it. He im-

mediately went the circuit and began to recount

his story completed by the happy climax. He

triumphed.

"What grieved me so much was not the thing

itself, as the lying. There is nothing so shameful

as to be placed under a cloud on account of a

lie."

He talked of his adventure all day long, he

told it on the highway to people who were pass-

ing by, in the inn to people who were drinking

there, and to persons coming out of church the

following Sunday. He stopped strangers to tell

them about it. He was calm now, and yet something disturbed him without his knowing ex-
actly what it was. People had the air of joking
while they listened. They did not seem con-
vinced. He seemed to feel that remarks were
being made behind his back.

On Tuesday of the next week he went to the
market at Goderville, urged solely by the neces-
sity he felt of discussing the case.

Malandain, standing at his door, began to
laugh on seeing him pass. Why?

He approached a farmer from Criquetot, who

did not let him finish, and giving him a thump

in the stomach said to his face:

"You clever rogue."

Then he turned his back on him.

Maître Hauchecorne was confused, why was

he called a clever rogue?

When he was seated at the table, in Jour-

dain's tavern he commenced to explain "the

affair."

A horse dealer from Monvilliers called to

him:

"Come, come, old sharper, that's an old

trick; I know all about your piece of string!"

Hauchecorne stammered:

"But the pocket-book was found."

But the other man replied:

"Shut up, papa, there is one that finds, and there is one that brings back. No one is any the wiser, so you get out of it."

The peasant stood choking. He understood. They accused him of having had the pocket-book returned by a confederate, by an accomplice.

He tried to protest. All the table began to laugh.

He could not finish his dinner and went away, in the midst of jeers.

He went home ashamed and indignant, choking with anger and confusion, the more dejected that he was capable with his Norman cunning of doing what they had accused him of, and even of boasting of it as a good trick. His innocence seemed to him, in a confused way, impossible to prove, as his sharpness was known. And he was stricken to the heart by the injustice of the suspicion.

Then he began to recount the adventure again, enlarging his story every day, adding each time new reasons, more energetic protestations,

more solemn oaths which he imagined and pre-

pared in his hours of solitude, his whole mind

given up to the story of the string. He was be-

lieved so much the less as his defense was more

complicated and his arguing more subtle.

"Those are lying excuses," they said behind

his back.

He felt it, consumed his heart over it, and

wore himself out with useless efforts. He was

visibly wasting away.

The wags now made him tell about the string

to amuse them, as they make a soldier who has

been on a campaign tell about his battles. His
mind, seriously affected, began to weaken.

Towards the end of December he took to his
bed.

He died in the first days of January, and in
the delirium of his death struggles he kept
claiming his innocence, reiterating.

"A piece of string, a piece of string—look—
here it is."

~~~~~~~~~~~~~~~~~~~~~